W9-AQB-931

BATMAN
DARK KNIGHT
DYNASTY

Published by DC Comics

DC Comics, 1700 Broadway, New York, NY 10019
A division of Warner Bros.–A Time Warner Entertainment Company

Printed in Canada

Hardcover illustration by Brom
Softcover illustration by Scott Hampton

Hardcover ISBN: 1-56389-384-3
Softcover ISBN: 1-56389-390-8

Dark Knight Dynasty

Mike W. Barr
Writer

Dark Past:

Scott Hampton
Painter

John Costanza
Letterer

Dark Present:

Gary Frank
Cam Smith
Artists

Ian Hannin
Alex Bleyaert
Robert Ro
Color and Separations

Ken Lopez
Letterer

Dark Future:

Scott McDaniel
Bill Sienkiewicz
Artists

Matt Hollingsworth
Colorist

Jean Munroe
James Rochelle
Separations

Richard Starkings~
Comicraft
Computer Letterer

For Dick Sprang
and the memory of Bill Finger
and Gardner Fox, in whose shadows
we all labor—MWB

To my fellow rail barons:
Mark Kneece, Paul Young, Durwin Talon,
Karen Hankala and
"Perfidious" Bob Pendarvist—SH

For William and Mia—GF

For my wife, Biz, without whom
I wouldn't do what I do—CS

I have dedicated this work to God
for giving me the talent,
and to my wife Amy
and son Alex for encouraging
me to develop it—SM

In memory of Lou Stathis
and Stan Drake—BS

In Elseworlds, heroes are taken from their usual settings and put into strange times and places—some that have existed or might have existed, and others that can't, couldn't or shouldn't exist. The result is stories that make characters who are as familiar as yesterday seem as fresh as tomorrow.

DARK PAST

London, England:
A.D. 1222.
BRING FORTH THE ACCUSED.
IMMEDIATELY, YOUR GRACE.

ON YOUR FEET, MY FINE KNIGHT TEMPLAR...

...THE ARCHBISHOP HIMSELF HAS DECIDED TO HEAR YOUR CONFESSION!
WELL?

MORE PARCHMENT.

pains me that you and I have
grown apart since the death of you
sainted mother on her pilgrimage these
many years agone. Yet I do not
regret casting my allegiance with the
Knights Templar, for through their good
offices I have been able to further the
will of God. Yet I sense the end of
many things is near, and wish to
communicate with you once again. On
the peril of my soul, the story I have
communicated herein is true, and I
pray to the Author of All Truths that
you will believe it.
There are many, I fear,
who do not.
Your loving
Father,
Joshua of Wainwright

NO MORE WRITING. NOW IT'S TIME FOR A BATH!

NO!
--MY PAPERS...!
JOSHUA, MY SON...
WHO--?

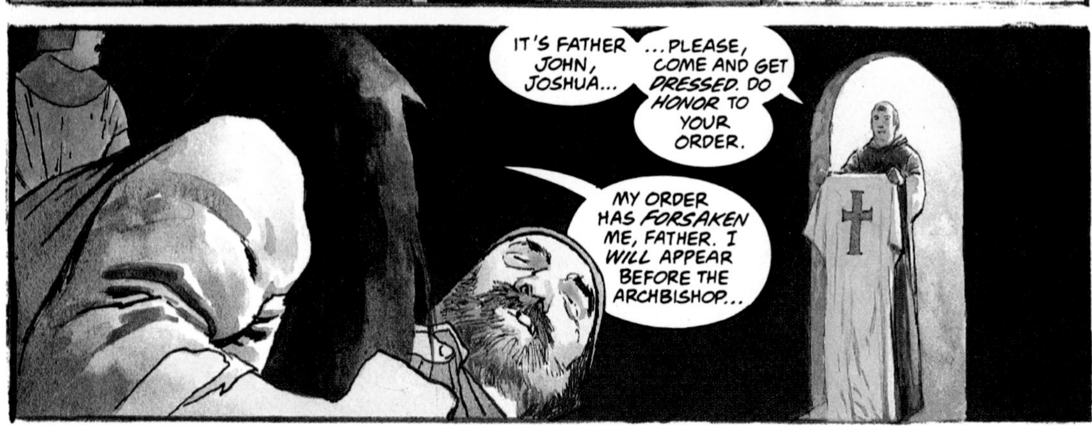
IT'S FATHER JOHN, JOSHUA...
...PLEASE, COME AND GET DRESSED. DO HONOR TO YOUR ORDER.
MY ORDER HAS FORSAKEN ME, FATHER. I WILL APPEAR BEFORE THE ARCHBISHOP...

"... But only in my family's coat of arms."
IS THIS *SUITABLE* TO YOU, JOSHUA? IS YOUR *PRIDE* SATISFIED?
THIS GOES *BEYOND* PRIDE, FATHER. WHY I CANNOT HERE *EXPLAIN*...

... BUT THESE *PAPERS* WILL TELL THE TALE. WILL YOU SEE THAT *WILLIAM* RECEIVES THEM? THESE AND THE OTHER POSSESSIONS THE COURT HAS *STRIPPED* FROM ME?
OF COURSE, MY SON.

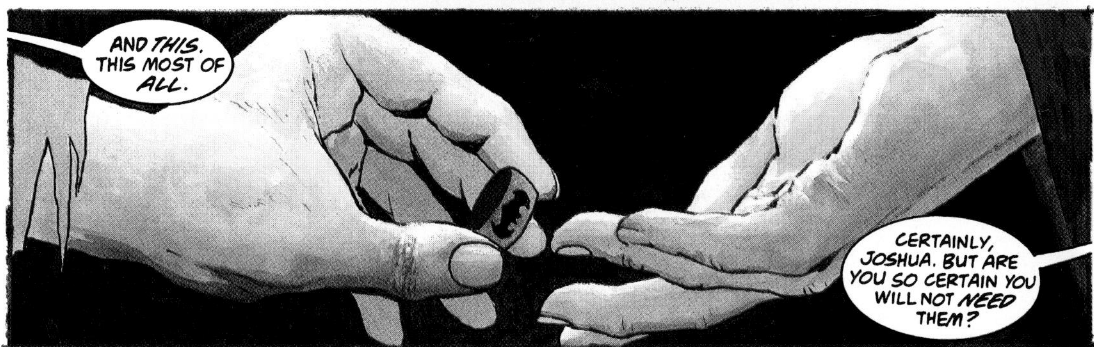

MAKE HASTE, YOU! THE ARCHBISHOP IS WAITING!

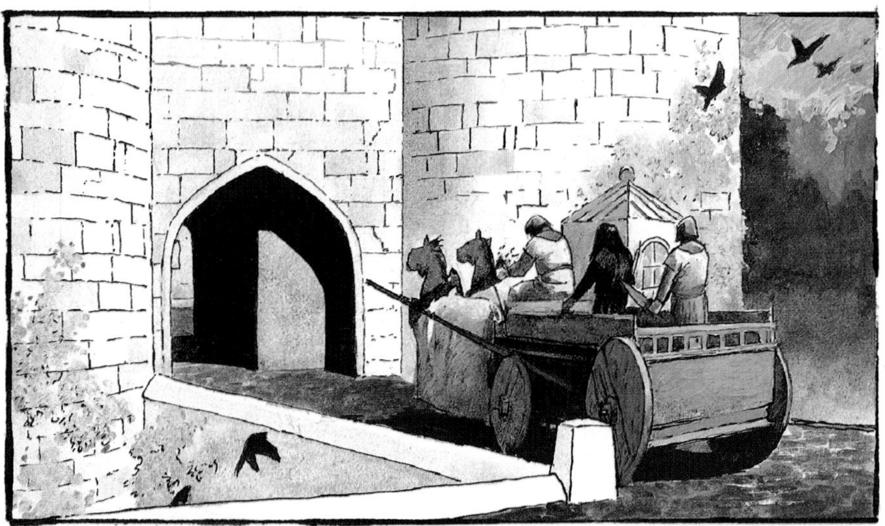

YOU ARE JOSHUA OF WAINWRIGHT?
I AM.

THE CHARGES AGAINST YOU ARE MOST GRAVE, SIR JOSHUA--YOU WOULD DO WELL TO PAY THIS COUNCIL THE RESPECT IT IS DUE, BY PROPERLY ADDRESSING US AND STANDING BEFORE US!
I SHOULD LIKE NOTHING BETTER, YOUR GRACE...

...BUT AS YOU MAY BE AWARE, I WAS HOBBLED WHEN I FIRST ENTERED YOUR CARE--AND THE HOSPITALITY OF YOUR INQUISITORS HAS DONE NOTHING TO IMPROVE MY CONDITION.
THEY ARE SERVANTS OF THE LORD, EVEN AS WE ARE, SIR JOSHUA...

YOU MAY *PROCEED*, SIR JOSHUA--BUT REMEMBER, WE ARE CONCERNED ONLY WITH THE RELEVANT *TRUTHS*.

AS AM I, YOUR GRACE--INDEED, A DESIRE TO KNOW THE TRUTH, TO DO GOD'S *WILL*, WAS THE REASON I *BECAME* A KNIGHT OF THE TEMPLE, AFTER THE DEATH OF MY DEAR *MARTHA*.

MY ONLY REGRET IS THAT THIS MOST RECENT CRUSADE DID NOT SUCCEED IN WRESTING THE HOLY LAND FROM THE GRIP OF THE *PAGANS* THAT HAVE HELD THEM FOR FAR TOO LONG...

"... But I was content to do God's will in other work as the Temple commanded me, while praying for a sixth crusade that would finally liberate the lands that birthed our savior.

"My services, and those of four other fine knights, were required to convey some gold to be ransomed for the lives of some unfortunate PILGRIMS who had been captured by PAGANS.

"Word of our campaign quickly SPREAD, despite our efforts to the opposite, and it was not only the PAGANS who coveted our gold."

COME, BROTHERS! LET US MAKE THEM PAY FOR THEIR CRIME!
UNDER OTHER CIRCUM-STANCES, I MIGHT AGREE WITH YOU, BROTHER MATTHEW...

...BUT THOSE BANDITS HAVE LEARNED THEIR LESSON, I THINK, AND THOSE PILGRIMS HAVE ALREADY WAITED TOO LONG!
YOU ARE RIGHT, BROTHER JOSHUA! IS THE RANSOM SECURE, BROTHER PAUL?
AS SAFE AS IN ITS MOTHER'S ARMS--OR AT LEAST, IN MY MOTHER'S ARMS!

THEN LET US AWAY. WE MUST SOON MAKE CAMP FOR THE NIGHT...
...AND I WOULD SLEEP WITHOUT THE STENCH OF CAR-RION IN MY DREAMS!

"We encamped some miles further away than I had intended, partook of our evening meal and said our Vesper prayers.

"The night was cool and still, yet alive with celestial beauty. Despite this display of God's power, I was of a mood which oft produces in me a certain MELAN-CHOLY...

"...Nor did it fail in its task tonight. My thoughts turned to my beloved wife, dead these many long years. I remembered the smell of her hair, the curve of her skin.
"For seeming hours did I dwell...
"...until I recalled my duties to the LIVING. I bid my men wake me for the second watch and retired.
"Better I had not slept at ALL, than to have seen the DREAM. Only LATER did all its elements coalesce into REASON...
"...At the time of its birth, it seemed to be my fall into MADNESS!
"At first I thought that which AWOKE me to be a part of my dream also...
YOU HAVE SLEPT TOO LONG, MY HUSBAND. BETTER YOU SHOULD RETURN TO THE LIVING.
MARTHA...?

MARTHA!
NO!

I AM SORRY! I COULD NOT RESIST! I DID NOT MEAN TO WAKE HIM--!
"She seemed to speak to someone, but no one but I was near! I had never encountered dementia like this outside of a DREAM...

"...So still did I suppose I dwelt in the land of Morpheus! I attempted to WAKE myself...

"...only to find I WAS awake! I HAD seen her! My Martha did LIVE!

"I could see no sign of her in the pre-dawn twilight. I sought the watch officer, to summon aid in my search...
BROTHER MATTHEW? MATTHEW!?

WHAT!?

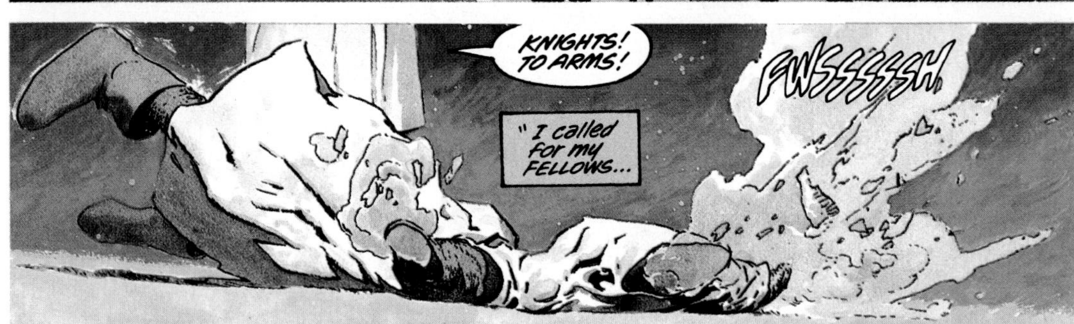
KNIGHTS! TO ARMS!
FWSSSSSSH
"I called for my FELLOWS...

"...only to find they could no longer HEAR me.
"All were DEAD, and the GOLD gone. I did not know HOW this had happened...

"...But as I saw that which the rising SUN did reveal, I knew...

"...That the mysteries around me were only BEGINNING to unfold!
"Where only solid rock had sat the night before, now stood a fully-formed CASTLE. You may think me a victim of my own DELUSIONS, your graces...
"...But it was as real as you, or as I, or as the love of GOD. This I do SWEAR.
"And if it took six full days for the LORD to create the universe, how could mortal man raise such a structure in mere HOURS?
"He could NOT, of course-- not without aid from a source whose name I feared to utter.

"If further proof were needed that my troubles emanated from this hellish structure, the foot-marks left by my Martha led to this strange castle...

"...or at least, to the edge of its surrounding MOAT.

"My first temptation was to immediately FOLLOW. But I did pray for the strength to RESIST this whim...

"...And thank the Lord that I was GRANTED such forbearance.
H'SSSSS

"It may have been simply the vaporous delusions of my mind that made me feel I was being WATCHED as I departed. But given the occurrences of the previous NIGHT...
"...I rather thought NOT.

"Mounting my assault on the cliffs BEHIND the castle took the better share of the day...

"...still, it was the only thing resembling a weak point in the structure's defenses. I prepared my supplies, ate, prayed, and waited for NIGHT...

"...Then I made READY.

"I tried again to pray, but I found my thoughts turning only to my MARTHA, and what her fate might be, how she may be SUFFERING.
"perhaps that was itself a kind of prayer.

"At any rate, I have always believed that prayers come to NOUGHT...

"...Unless married to ACTIONS.

"I confess, I kept my EYES closed.

"Until finally...

SHUFF!
WHUFFT!
WHUFFT!
UNFF

WHUFFT!

"I could not allow myself the luxury of nursing my wounds.

"For I felt I would not long be unmolested. My every instinct was to attack these minions of the devil's lair...

"...Then it OCCURRED--they wished to attain the castle interior to alert their FELLOWS...
"And I ALSO wished to attain the interior--but for a DIFFERENT reason.

"They seemed to have little knowledge of the ways of WAR.

"I therefore thought my victory to be easily OBTAINED...

"...Then I was reminded that NOTHING of value in this world comes easily...

"... And my newfound foes...

"... were not spawned by the will of GOD!

"The things had no souls, yet they were still controlled by the life behind those evil EYES...

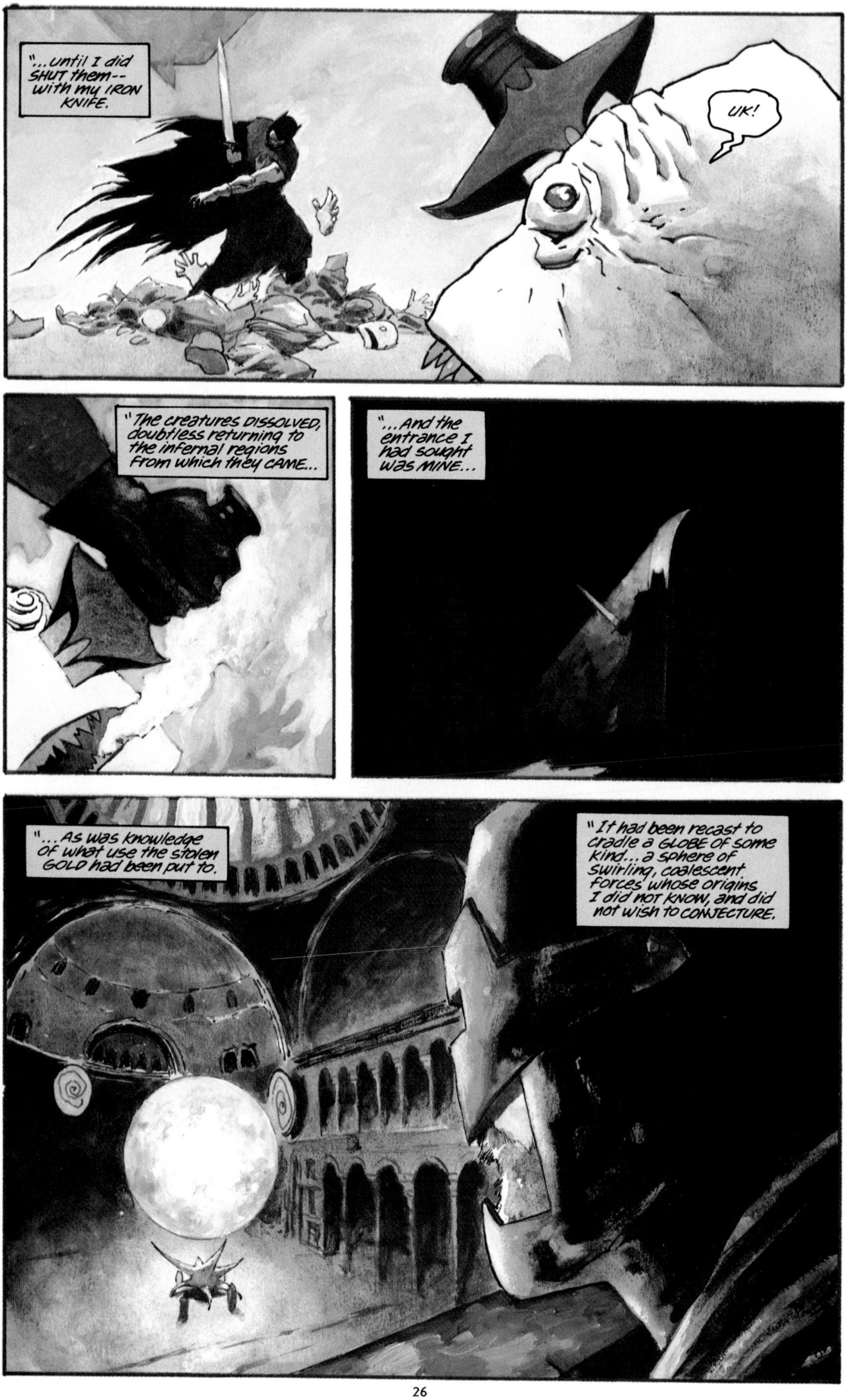

"...As was knowledge of what use the stolen GOLD had been put to.

"It had been recast to cradle a GLOBE of some kind... a sphere of swirling, coalescent forces whose origins I did not KNOW, and did not wish to CONJECTURE.

"My only desire, on seeing it, was to DESTROY it. But such an assault before RECONNAISSANCE would be the worst FOLLY.

:SNIFF: HE'S HERE...!
AND WHO IS "HE", MY DEAR?

N-NO ONE...
SALOMINA...!
WELL, ONE OF THOSE SILLY KNIGHTS, ACTUALLY.
A FIFTH? YOU TOLD THE SORCERERS THERE WERE ONLY FOUR.

YOU NEVER PAY ANY ATTENTION TO ME! I NEVER HAVE ANYONE TO TALK TO! LET ME KEEP HIM, PLEASE...!
HE ACTUALLY MADE IT THIS FAR...HMMM...

THEN I CAN HAVE HIM? OH, THANK YOU...!
JUST CAPTURE HIM, SALOMINA-- THEN WE'LL SEE.

IS SOMEONE THERE? PLEASE, HELP ME...!
"That VOICE. For years, I had heard it only in my DREAMS, until last NIGHT...

"...And until NOW.
MARTHA!?
JOSHUA! I KNEW GOD WOULD LEAD YOU TO ME!

BUT HOW DID YOU COME TO--?
DOES IT MATTER? HURRY, BELOVED... FREE ME!

YES, DEAREST! A MOMENT, AND--?
USE YOUR SWORD, JOSHUA, PLEASE-- NOT THAT KNIFE!
"So euphorious was I that I almost COMPLIED with her plea! Then I REMEMBERED all that had OCCURRED...

"...And the effect my knife's IRON blade did have upon the minions I fought EARLIER!
MARTHA, WHY ARE YOU SO AFRAID?
JOSHUA, NO! TAKE IT AWAY--!

DAMN YOU, JOSHUA OF WAINWRIGHT...!

...WHY COULDN'T YOU LEAVE WELL ENOUGH ALONE?
WHO ARE--?

YOU HAVE FAILED, SALOMINA... AS I FEARED.
NO! I COULD HAVE TURNED HIM!

MY DEAR...

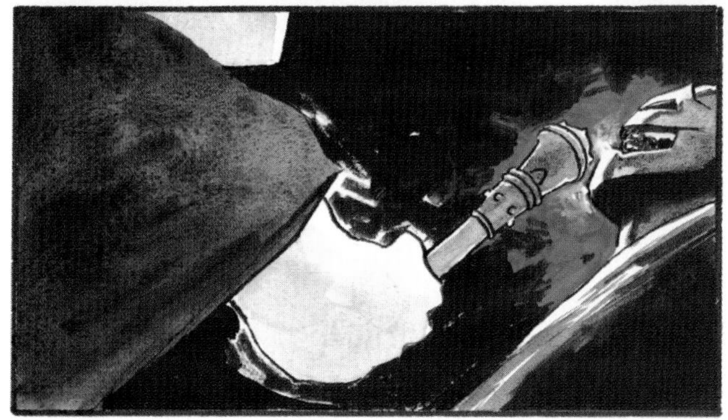

...YOU'LL FORGIVE ME IF I DOUBT THAT.

UNHHHH
HE'S BACK.
WHO... ARE YOU? WHAT IS YOUR PURPOSE HERE? AND --
AND WHY HAVE I NOT SLAIN YOU? AS TO THE FIRST, MY NAME IS VANDAL SAVAGE. AS TO THE SECOND, NONE OF YOUR AFFAIR. AS TO THE THIRD...
...I CONFESS, I AM INTRIGUED BY YOUR RESOLVE--YOUR RESOURCEFULNESS--AS I HAVE BEEN BY NO OTHER MAN'S... AND I'VE KNOWN MANY MEN IN MY TIME.
YOU DID NOT SPARE MY LIFE BECAUSE YOU WERE INTRIGUED!
WELL, I DID, IN A WAY. YOU LIVE BECAUSE I WISH YOU TO SERVE ME. AS MY GENERAL, MY WARLORD... WHATEVER YOU FEEL LIKE CALLING YOURSELF.
NEVER!
"NEVER," YOU SAY. "NOT EVER." ONLY I KNOW WHAT THAT PHRASE TRULY MEANS. NOTHING IS "NEVER."
ALMOST NOTHING.
SALOMINA.
YES, VANDAL?

YOU HAVE A NEW TOY. AMUSE YOURSELF, BUT REMEMBER-- HE IS MINE.
I KNOW WHAT YOU WANT, VANDAL...

... AND YOU KNOW WHAT I WANT!
QUITE WELL, SALOMINA--

--BUT I MAKE IT A HABIT NEVER TO MATE OUTSIDE MY SPECIES.
WHY DID YOU GIVE ME THE CAPACITY TO LOVE IF YOU WON'T LET ME USE IT?

"For the first time I thought I might perceive a GAP in this savage's armor...
LISTEN TO ME! FREE ME AND YOU MAY TAKE REVENGE UPON SAVAGE AND--

I WOULD RATHER EXAMINE THIS LOCKET, MY KNIGHT. IT SO FASCINATED ME LAST NIGHT...!
REPLACE THAT, WITCH, OR--

YOU WONDER WHY YOU WERE SPARED.
YOU WOULD DEEM IT "GOD'S WILL"... BUT IN TRUTH, I FOUND YOUR ASPECT COMELY...

...AND MY ASPECT CAN BE WHATEVER I SO CHOOSE--EVEN THAT OF YOUR MOST BELOVED.
NO...
"It was my MARTHA, once again young and strong and BEAUTIFUL.

OH, YES...!
"...And WARM and SOFT, and--

STOP! YOU ARE NOT HER!
BUT I CAN BE...

...I CAN GIVE YOU EVERY PASSION SHE EVER DID! ANY PLEASURE, ANY JOY--

ANY BUT THOSE OF THE SOUL--AND IT WAS HER SOUL I DID MOST LOVE.

YOU MEN! WHY DO YOU ALWAYS WANT WHAT YOU CAN NEVER HAVE?
KRAK
"Her blow must have carried a force that was PRETERNATURAL, for I lost my senses...

"...But when I regained this world, the madness seemed only to have increased!
YOU SHOULD HAVE ACCEPTED SALOMINA'S LOVE, SIR KNIGHT-- I'M AFRAID MY METHOD WILL BE RATHER LESS PLEASANT!

HOW MANY TIMES MUST I SAY IT--NEVER! I WILL ⁝KAFF⁝ BURN IN HELL BEFORE I--
ACTUALLY, YOU WILL BURN HERE. I WONDER, WILL YOU ROAST IN YOUR ARMOR OR CHOKE, OR WILL YOUR OWN WEIGHT PULL AN ARM OFF FIRST?

COME, SALOMINA, THE HOUR APPROACHES, AND WE HAVE MUCH TO DO.
BUT... SHOULD HE BE LEFT ALONE?

MY DEAR SALOMINA! UNLIKE EITHER YOU OR ME...
...HE'S ONLY HUMAN!

RRRRRPPPP

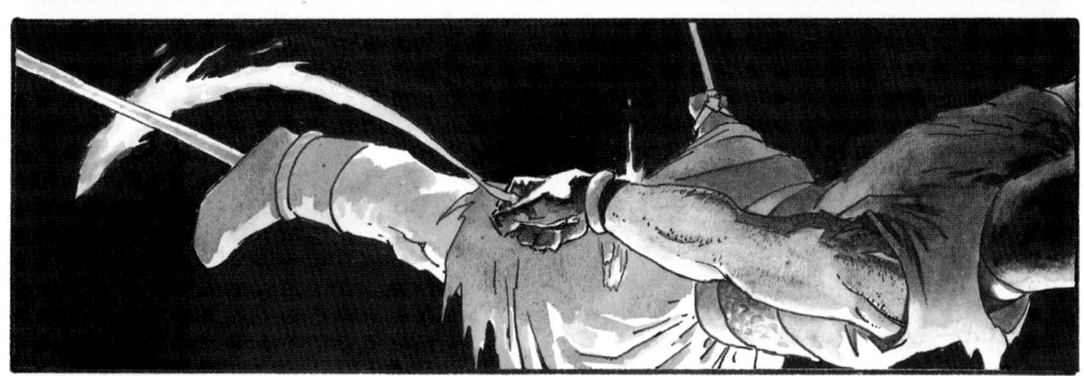

WHUD!
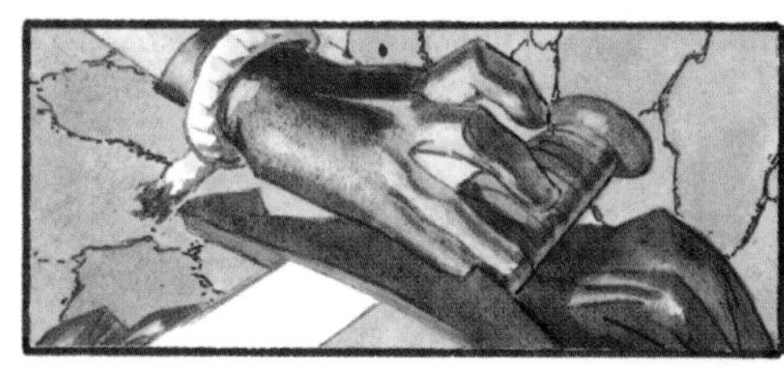
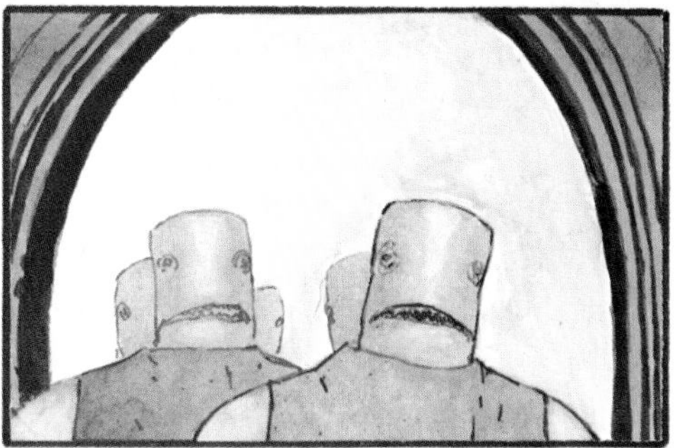

"My good KNIFE seemed effective against these abominations earlier. But with no oppor-tunity to wield it...

"...The sole remaining treatment that seemed to AVAIL...

"...was the cleansing breath of FLAME.

"I knew not what deviltry the Savage had PLANNED, I knew only that I must STOP it. To that end, I chose my MEANS...

KRAK

"...which also granted me OPPORTUNITY."

HERE YOU ARE! QUICKLY, TAKE YOUR PLACE!
"I stood on one side of the hellish sphere, and, gazing up at it...

"...I dimly began to understand WHAT the Savage wanted-- though not WHY...

"...But the cost of his machinations was clear to see!
BEGIN THE INCANTATION, FRATER MONTCLAIR... FRATER MONTCLAIR?

I MIGHT HAVE KNOWN.

GUARDS, SLAY HIM.

"Despite my best efforts--and my use of the KNIFE--the abominations got the better of me.

"And I swear, your graces, I would not be here now...

"...Had not the Lord sent a portion of the fire that led his people to the PROMISED LAND.

REMARKABLE--
TOTALLY *UNACCEPTABLE,*
BUT *REMARKABLE.*
SALOMINA.

BUT DO IT QUICKLY.
YES. IT WILL BE FAST.

RRRRARRGGH
AKKKK--!

RROOWWRR

M-MERCY...!

NO.

STOP HIM, JOSHUA :kaff: BEFORE HE-- HE--
STOP HIM.

:HKKKK:
SSLSSSSHH

OH, IT'S YOU.

HOW... HOW CAN YOU BE SLAIN, EVIL ONE?
"EVIL"? ALL I SEEK IS KNOWLEDGE...

...A FEW OF YOUR BRIEF, PETTY LIVES IS WORTH THAT!
AGGGGH--!
"None of my blows caused him grief! It was all I could do to save my OWN life...

"...Then I KNEW! If nothing of MY doing could harm him...
WHAT ARE YOU--?

"...perhaps his own craft could do him ill!
NOOOOO--!
"I am as certain as I am of my SALVATION that nothing within that castle could have survived that inferno...

JOSHUA, HERE... YOU KNOW, I-- I...

I KNOW, SALOMINA...

...IN ANOTHER LIFE, I MIGHT HAVE FELT LIKEWISE.

...AND, AFTER NO LITTLE TRAVAIL, I MADE MY WAY BACK TO ENGLAND, WHERE I HAVE BEEN IMPRISONED THESE LONG MONTHS! I AM INNOCENT OF THE CHARGES, YOUR GRACES, AND I BEG YOU TO SET ME FREE.
"INNOCENT," SIR JOSHUA? WITHOUT PROOF, ALL WE KNOW...

...IS THAT THE MEN AND GOLD YOU EMBARKED WITH HAVE VANISHED, WITH THE PILGRIMS YOU WERE SENT TO RANSOM! UNLESS YOU RECANT AND EMBRACE THE FAITH, YOU MUST PAY THE PENALTY!
I RECANT NOTHING--!

I AM INNO--
NO! IT CANNOT BE!

YOU KNEW OF THE GOLD'S TRANSPORT... AND COVETED IT FOR YOURSELF! TO INCREASE YOUR WEALTH--!
NO, NO, TO AID MY SPELL-- THE SPELL THAT DREW YOU TO THAT AREA. GENIUS IS IN THE DETAILS.

I WILL-- NNNGGG!
YOU WON'T. NO ONE CAN.

I WIN AGAIN.

sigh
I ALWAYS WIN.

Dark Present

ON OCCASIONS LIKE THESE IT'S A FAMILY TRADITION TO TOAST THE MEMORY OF A FAVORITE WAYNE ANCESTOR. SO HERE'S TO JOSHUA OF WAINWRIGHT...

...AND, OF COURSE, TO MY MOTHER AND FATHER...
...AND MY BEAUTIFUL BRIDE, JULIE.
YES, OLD JOSHUA WAS ONE OF THOSE KNIGHTS TEMPLAR, BURNED AT THE STAKE FOR SOME SORT OF HERESY AND ALL THAT... AN INTERESTING FELLOW, I IMAGINE.
YES, HE WAS.
WHAT WAS THAT, VALENTIN?
I SAID "I'M SURE HE WAS"--AN INTERESTING FELLOW, THAT IS.
VALENTIN, I DON'T THINK YOU'VE HAD THE PLEASURE. JULIE MADISON--ER, JULIE WAYNE, MR. VALENTIN SINCLAIR. DAD'S RIGHT-HAND MAN AT WAYNETECH.
CONGRATULATIONS, MRS. WAYNE. MAY I PRESENT MS. JENNA CLARK?
AND THIS IS THE OLD SLAVE-DRIVER HIMSELF, JENNA--AND MRS. WAYNE.
DON'T BELIEVE A WORD OF IT, MS. CLARK! VALENTIN IS THE ONE WHO CRACKS THE WHIP!
THOMAS COULDN'T RUN WAYNETECH WITHOUT HIM!
I SEE. SO NICE TO MEET YOU BOTH...

...WE MUST KEEP IN TOUCH.

MIND IF I CUT IN?
I DON'T KNOW, DAD--CAN I TRUST YOU WITH HER?
THE QUESTION IS, CAN YOU TRUST ME WITH HIM?

THERE'S SOMETHING I'LL BET YOU THOUGHT YOU'D NEVER SEE, MOM--DAD DANCING WITH HIS DAUGHTER-IN-LAW.
JULIE IS WONDERFUL, BRUCE! I'M SO HAPPY FOR YOU!

...HAVE YOU GIVEN ANY THOUGHT TO WHAT YOU'LL BE DOING AFTER THE HONEY-MOON?
NOT A THING.

YOU KNOW, YOUR FATHER WOULD LOVE IT IF YOU TOOK MORE OF AN INTEREST IN WAYNETECH...
I DO KNOW IT, MOM. AND I MAY...

...BUT NOT TONIGHT!

SAVE US!

DON'T LET US DIE!

STOP GOLIATH!

JULIE, GET BACK--!

"TAKE YOUR TIME," SAYS MY HUSBAND, WHILE HE WATCHES TV? THAT'LL FILL A NEW BRIDE WITH CONFIDENCE...!

JULIE, HUSH.

...THIS IS THE WAYNETECH SHUTTLE INTERCEPTOR, IN POSITION, GOTHAM BASE. AWAITING SIGNAL TO HATCH THE EGG.

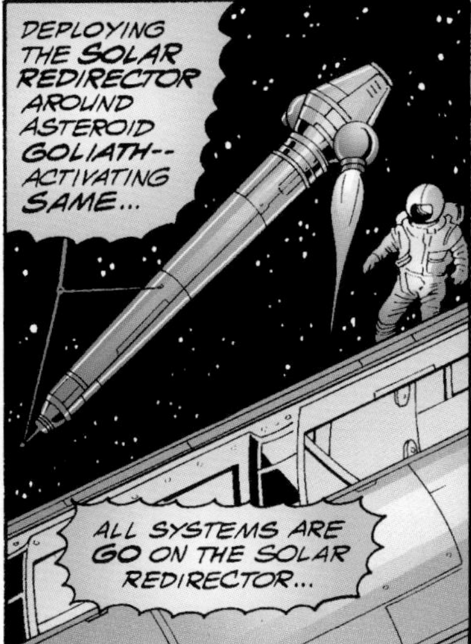

...IT'S A GO, GOTHAM BASE! DO YOU READ? IT'S A GO! THE REFLECTOR IS CATCHING THE SUN...

...AND VAPORIZING THE ASTEROID! THAT MASS CHANGE SHOULD SEND GOLIATH BACK INTO SPACE, MISSING MOTHER EARTH BY A WIDE MARGIN! DO YOU READ?

WE READ YOU, INTERCEPTOR...!

...WE READ!

DID YOU SEE IT, JULIE?
I SAW IT, DARLING! THE EARTH IS SAFE FOR US...

...AND FOR OUR CHILDREN.
YES...

...OUR CHILDREN.

IS IT TIME, VANDAL?
MORE THAN YOU KNOW, JENNA...

...MORE THAN YOU KNOW.
TAP TAP TAP

WILL YOU AND MRS. WAYNE BE NEEDING ANYTHING ELSE TONIGHT, SIR?
NO, THANK YOU, ALFRED-- WE'LL SEE YOU IN THE MORNING.

A LITTLE SOMETHING TO HELP YOU SLEEP, MARTHA? THOUGH AFTER A DAY LIKE THIS ONE, I DON'T KNOW THAT I'LL NEED IT...
HMM? I'M SORRY, DEAR, WHAT WERE YOU SAYING...?

YOU WERE THINKING ABOUT BRUCE, WEREN'T YOU?
YES. I SO HOPE HE'S HAPPY...

...I HOPE HE CAN FIND WHATEVER HE'S SOUGHT ALL HIS LIFE.

IF HE DOESN'T, IT WON'T BE FROM LACK OF YOUR TRYING. PERHAPS HE'S JUST A LATE BLOOMER. YOU SPOIL HIM, YOU KNOW.
I SPOIL HIM?

THOMAS... WHY DON'T WE GO TO BED...?
IN A MINUTE, DEAR...
...FIRST, JUST LET ME CHECK--
--GOOD LORD, NO...!
THOMAS, WHAT IS IT?

THE ANGLE OF THE DEFLECTOR BEAM HAS BEEN CHANGED! IF LEFT IN THAT POSITION, GOLIATH WILL BE PROPELLED TO STRIKE THE EARTH--AND EVEN MORE FORCEFULLY!
THOMAS, THAT CAN'T BE! SURELY SOMEONE ELSE WOULD HAVE NOTICED!
HELLO, THOMAS...?

VALENTIN, THE ANGLE OF THE DEFLECTOR BEAM HAS BEEN CHANGED!
ARE YOU SURE?
IT MAY BE A PROBLEM WITH THE SOFTWARE. DON'T MENTION THIS TO ANYONE ELSE--I'LL BE RIGHT OVER!

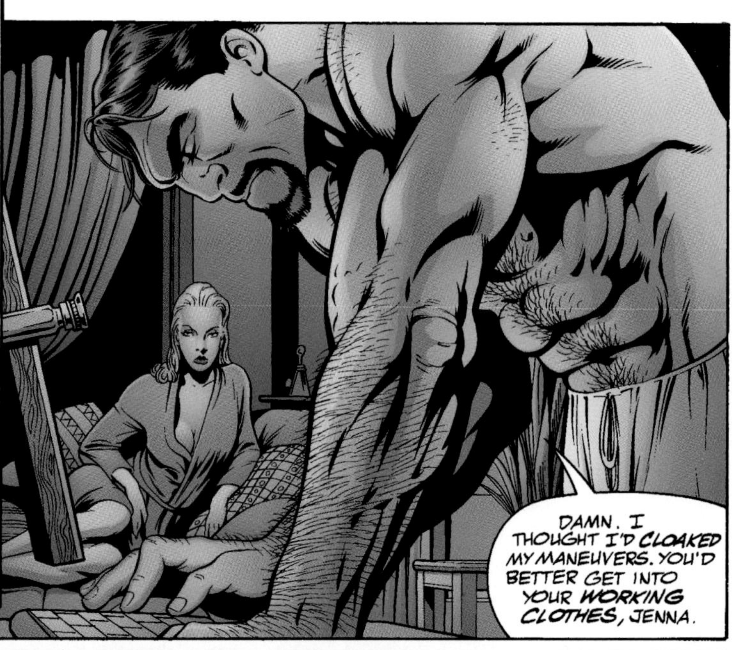
DAMN. I THOUGHT I'D CLOAKED MY MANEUVERS. YOU'D BETTER GET INTO YOUR WORKING CLOTHES, JENNA.

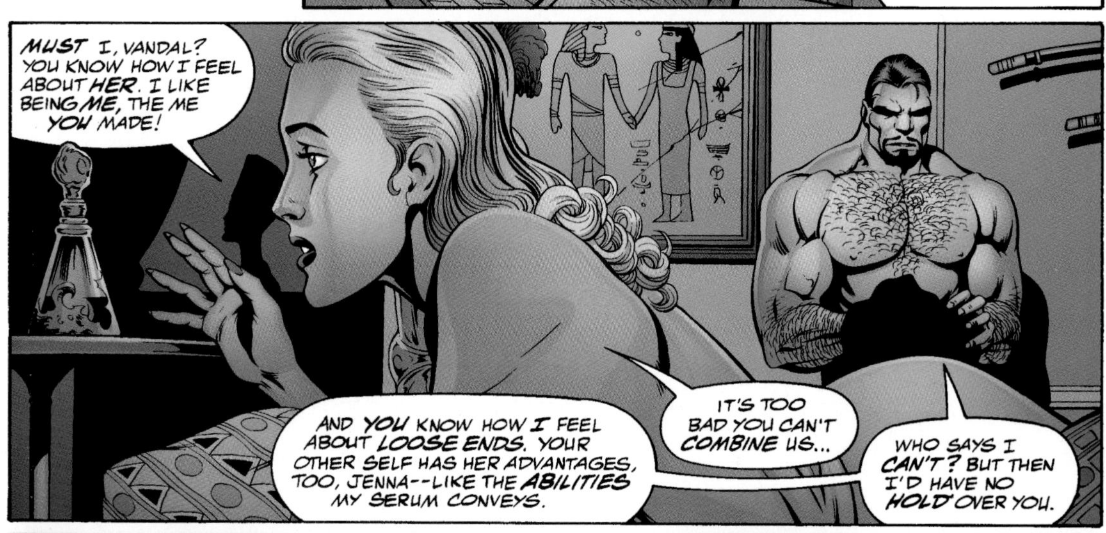
MUST I, VANDAL? YOU KNOW HOW I FEEL ABOUT HER. I LIKE BEING ME, THE ME YOU MADE!
AND YOU KNOW HOW I FEEL ABOUT LOOSE ENDS. YOUR OTHER SELF HAS HER ADVANTAGES, TOO, JENNA--LIKE THE ABILITIES MY SERUM CONVEYS.
IT'S TOO BAD YOU CAN'T COMBINE US...
WHO SAYS I CAN'T? BUT THEN I'D HAVE NO HOLD OVER YOU.

SIGH I'D HOPED THIS DAY WOULD NEVER COME. IT SEEMS ONLY YESTERDAY THAT I--
WELL, NO MATTER. ARE YOU READY, JENNA?

I'M AFRAID SO.

VALENTIN?
HOW DID YOU GET THIS FAR WITHOUT--?
WE'VE NO TIME TO DISCUSS BUILDING SECURITY, THOMAS.

...WE HAVE TO DEAL WITH THIS NOW. HAVE YOU TOLD ANYONE ELSE?
N-NO...IF IT GOT OUT, IT COULD CAUSE PANIC.
HOW CONSIDERATE.
WHAT ARE YOU DOING--!? YOU CAN'T--
DELETE FILE
YOU'D BE SURPRISED WHAT I CAN DO. FOR EXAMPLE THIS--THOUGH I TRULY AM SORRY.
JENNA...

...MAKE IT LOOK LIKE AN ACCIDENT.
I TOUCHED THEM, REMEMBER? I'M INSIDE THEM, IN THEIR MINDS, IN THEIR SOULS.
IT WILL MORE THAN "LOOK" LIKE ONE...

WHAT CAUSES MORE ACCIDENTS THAN SIMPLE, PRIMAL FEAR?
STOP THAT...WHAT ARE YOU--?

THOMAS, WHERE ARE WE? IS THIS REAL?
I DON'T KNOW, I--
OH, NO.
THIS IS A STICKUP...
THE MARK OF ZORRO

...I'LL TAKE THAT NECKLACE YOU'RE WEARIN', LADY!
THOMAS, RUN--!

RUUUNNN!

WHAT DO YOU SUPPOSE THEY SAW?
OH, I HAVE A FEELING I KNOW...
THUDDT
WRRRINCH

YOU'VE DONE WELL, JENNA--OR SHOULD I CALL YOU THE "SCARECRONE"?
I HATE THAT NAME--BUT I'M NOT JENNA! VANDAL, YOU KNOW WHAT I WANT!

OH, YOU MEAN THIS...?
OOPS BUTTER-FINGERS.
NO--!

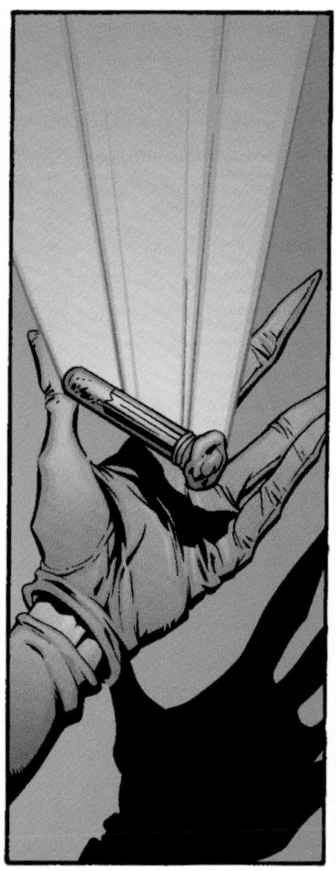

YOU DIRTY--
JENNA...

...I BELIEVE WE'VE OVERSTAYED OUR WELCOME.

MASTER WAYNE? MRS. WAYNE? I THOUGHT I HEARD--

BRINN..
HELLO?
MASTER BRUCE...
ALFRED, I APPRECIATE THE CONCERN, BUT...

...THERE'S BEEN AN ACCIDENT.
BRUCE, WHAT'S WRONG--?

UH...EXCUSE US, MISTER WAYNE...

...BUT WE'VE GOT TO--
NO! NO ONE TOUCHES THEM! DO YOU UNDERSTAND?

BRUCE-- THEY HAVE A JOB TO DO?
YOU DON'T WANT PHOTOGRAPHERS ALL AROUND...
NO. YOU'RE RIGHT. SORRY, COMMISSIONER.

WE FIGURE THEY FELL, BRUCE. LOST THEIR BALANCE. THERE'S NO INDICATION OF FOUL PLAY.
"FELL"? THEY LIVED HERE FOR YEARS. WHAT WOULD CAUSE THEM TO FALL?

THE SAME CAUSE OF THE SEVEN OTHER FATAL FALLS SUFFERED THIS WEEK, BRUCE-- PEOPLE LOOKING AT THE SKY, AND LOSING THEIR FOOTING.
STILL, IT'S SO UNLIKE DAD...

BUT HERE'S THE CLINCHER. NONE OF THE LOBBY SECURITY CAMERAS OR COMPUTER LOGS SHOW ANY UNAUTHORIZED ENTRY OR SIGNS OF TAMPERING. NO ONE WAS UP HERE WHO SHOULDN'T HAVE BEEN.
BRUCE... I'M VERY SORRY.
YES...OF COURSE. THANK YOU.

EXCUSE ME, BRUCE...

...BUT I WANTED TO TELL YOU AGAIN HOW SORRY I AM. THOMAS AND MARTHA WERE DEAR FRIENDS.
YES... EVER SINCE YOU SCARED OFF THAT GUNMAN, YEARS AGO, AFTER THAT MOVIE... WHAT WAS IT WE SAW?

I DON'T REMEMBER, BRUCE. TAKE OFF AS MUCH TIME AS YOU LIKE. I'LL MIND THE OFFICE.
ONE LAST THING, VALENTIN--WOULD YOU MIND DROPPING JULIE OFF?
HONEY, WHY...?

I'VE GOT SOME WORK TO DO IN THE CITY, DARLING. SEE YOU LATER.
ALL RIGHT...

KEEP AN EYE ON YOUNG MR. WAYNE. MAKE SURE HE DOESN'T GO ANYPLACE THAT MIGHT ENDANGER HIM!
YES, SIR.

SHALL I PREPARE THE EVENING REPAST, MASTER BRUCE?
JUST COFFEE, ALFRED...

...THIS MAY BE A LONG NIGHT.

ALFRED!
IF YOU DESIRE MORE CAFFEINE, I SHALL HAVE TO SEND OUT TO COLOMBIA, SIR.

THE TIME CODE ON THIS TAPE! IT SAYS THIS TAPE OF THE WAYNE PENTHOUSE ELEVATOR WAS TAKEN AT 8:15-- JUST BEFORE MY PARENTS WERE KILLED!
SIR, I'M AFRAID I DON'T SEE--

BUT THE TAPE WAS ACTUALLY TAKEN MUCH EARLIER! THIS SECURITY TAPE HAS BEEN SUBSTITUTED FOR THE ACTUAL TAPE, ALFRED! THE KILLERS MUST HAVE COME IN BY THE ELEVATOR!
ENHANCE

JOSHUA OF WAINWRIGHT!

OF COURSE!

I SEE, SIR...

WAYNETECH

NO DELIVERIES BETWEEN 12-2 PM

MR. SINCLAIR--WE'VE GOT A BREAK-IN IN TAPE STORAGE. YOU WANTED TO BE TOLD--
A BREAK-IN?

...EVEN THOUGH THERE'S NOTHING TO FIND--IS THERE?
N-NO, SIR! THE TAPES I DUPED WERE DEAD PERFECT!

AND THAT'S HOW I WANT OUR INTRUDER. TAKE SOME OTHER MEN WITH YOU.
YESSIR!

WHAT'S THAT?

WHO SENT YOU?

AGGGG--!
ZINNNG
SPWEEE
HIS CAPE MUST BE BULLETPROOF!
YOU'RE SMART. SMART ENOUGH TO SURRENDER?
DENT
TRUCTION
KEEP
OUT!
KE
W--WE =PUFT= MADE IT...!
HOME FREE...!

THWPPT
WNNKT
RIVETS 1·5'
MUSTA LEFT...
UH, UH...!
IT'S HIM!
HELP--!

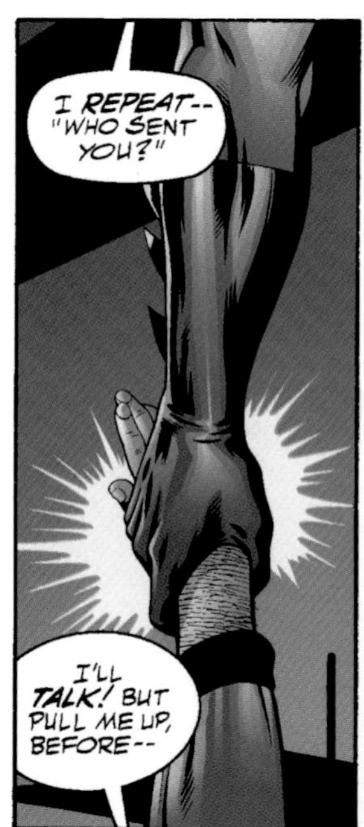

I REPEAT-- "WHO SENT YOU?"
I'LL TALK! BUT PULL ME UP, BEFORE--

WKNNT
CRRNG
AAAAAH!

SPTNNG
WNNNG

RMMMBLL

UNNNF

GET AWAY--!

LOOK OUT...!
WHOA!

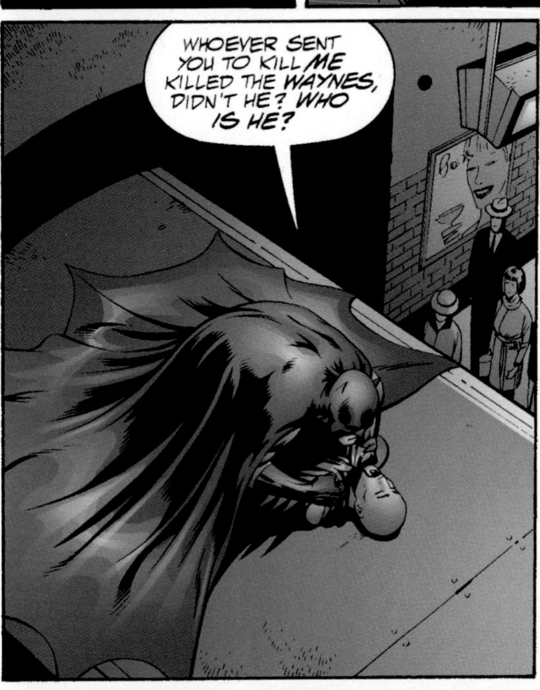
WHOEVER SENT YOU TO KILL ME KILLED THE WAYNES, DIDN'T HE? WHO IS HE?

S-SINCLAIR...!

...AND IN OTHER NEWS TODAY...
JENNA, WILL YOU PLEASE TURN THAT DRIVEL OFF?
...POLICE SEEM TO HAVE NO CLUE TO THE MYSTERIOUS ASSAILANT, DRESSED AS A BAT, WHO EARLIER TONIGHT...
A BAT?
VALENTIN, WHAT'S WRONG?
NOTHING, JENNA... AFTER ALL THESE YEARS, THE PORRIDGE OF LIFE HAS ATTAINED A PINCH OF SPICE. I SUGGEST YOU GET READY, WE MAY--
KREESH!
SINCLAIR! I KNOW EVERYTHING!
DO YOU, NOW?
WHY DID YOU HAVE THE WAYNES KILLED?
THEN YOU KNOW FAR LESS THAN "EVERYTHING," DON'T YOU... BRUCE?
HOW DID YOU--?
I SEE. ACTUALLY, YOU KNOW LESS THAN NOTHING.
JENNA?

DON'T CALL ME THAT.
WHAT ARE YOU--?

D-DON'T...!

IS THIS HOW YOU CARRY ON THE WAYNE TRADITION? BY DRESSING LIKE A WINGED RAT?
I ALWAYS KNEW HE'D FAIL US!
MOM... DAD... DON'T GO...!

...I WAS ALWAYS AFRAID I'D DISAPPOINT YOU... THAT I COULDN'T EVER...
...DON'T GO!

DO YOU KNOW WHAT HE FEARS, TOO?
I KNOW WHAT EVERYONE FEARS, JENNA. IT COMES FROM LONG EXPERIENCE WITH THE SPECIES.

HE COULD HAVE KILLED ME. WHY DIDN'T--?

KRA-WHOOOM
I'VE ADDED THIS LATEST DATA TO MY REPORT, SIR, BUT... ARE YOU CERTAIN? MR. SINCLAIR? IT SEEMS--
"OUTLANDISH"? "IMPOSSIBLE"? I AGREE, ALFRED, BUT HE'S UP TO SOMETHING INVOLVING THE SHUTTLE, AND--
THE FILES ON THIS COMPUTING DEVICE ARE QUITE SECURELY ENCODED, SIR. DO YOU HAVE ANY IDEA WHAT THIS DESIGN IS?
SOME KIND OF ENERGY WAVE, PERHAPS. KEEP WORKING ON IT, ALFRED, I'M TAKING--
HELLO?
BRUCE, IS EVERYTHING ALL RIGHT? I'M--
JUST SOME WAYNETECH STUFF, HONEY. ALFRED AND I ARE GOING TO BE AT IT FOR A WHILE YET...
...IT MIGHT BE MORE FUN FOR YOU IF YOU STAYED AT YOUR PARENTS' FOR A COUPLE OF--
BRUCE WAYNE, LISTEN TO ME!
IS IT ME? IS THERE SOMETHING WRONG WITH... WITH OUR MARRIAGE?
HONEY, NO...!

DRAT.
INCORRECT PASSWORD!

THEN WHAT? YOU'RE SO... SECRETIVE, LATELY. WHATEVER YOU'RE DOING, IT'S LIKE YOU'RE NO LONGER THE MAN I LOVE.
JULIE, BELIEVE ME...

BLAST.

...IF I DIDN'T DO WHAT I'M DOING, I WOULDN'T BE THE MAN YOU LOVE.
ONCE THIS IS ALL OVER, I'M YOURS. FOREVER.
OH, BRUCE...!

OH, MY WORD...!
5.
4.
3.

KRA-WHA-WHOOM
WHAT--?
ALFRED!

BRUCE, MAYBE HE--HE MIGHT--
NO.

HE'S GONE, JULIE--JUST LIKE MY PARENTS.
YOU'RE ALL I HAVE LEFT.

MR. SINCLAIR, THIS IS HIGHLY IRREGULAR...!
NONETHELESS, IN THE ABSENCE OF THOMAS WAYNE, I COMMAND WAYNETECH...

...AND THE MISSION IS ON. IS THAT CLEAR, MAJOR?
Y-YESSIR.

VALENTIN, IS THIS NECESSARY? BRUCE WAYNE IS DEAD--
BUT WHAT HE CAN LEARN, SO CAN ANOTHER. I APPRECIATED THE DIVERSION HE PROVIDED, TRUE...

...BUT IT'S TIME FOR ENDGAME.

HUUULLL--!

WHUD!

WILLIAMS, COME ALONG!
SORRY, MR. SINCLAIR!

--LIFTOFF!
WROOOM

WE'LL APPROACH THE DISH IN A FEW MINUTES. DON YOUR GRAVITY BOOTS, AND MAN YOUR--
--WHERE'S WILLIAMS?
MR. SINCLAIR...!

...WILLIAMS IS NOT HERE!
DAMN! WE HAVE A HOSTILE ABOARD! ALL OF YOU, FAN OUT AND--

MR. SINCLAIR? THE LIGHTS--!
YOU HAVE YOUR ORDERS--FIND HIM! USE THE EMERGENCY WEAPONS, NOT BALLISTICS! JENNA, GET READY!

"NEEDLE GUNS!" WISH I COULD USE MY .44.
NOT ABOARD A SPACECRAFT, YOU DON'T. HEY, THERE'S ONE PAIR OF GRAVITY BOOTS STILL HERE!
BUT THAT MEANS--

THAT MEANS I'M NOT WEARING ANY!

HE'S HERE!
CLUDDD!
TWO DOWN.
FWSSSH
HOLD IT--!
STAY STILL, AND I'LL DO IT QUICK!
I WOULDN'T.
YOU AIN'T ME.
FHSSSST

UNCONTAINED FIRE. INSTITUTING EMERGENCY VACUUM IN 5--4--
FWOOOSHT
AGGGH--!

FIRE EXTINGUISHED. ALERT CANCELLED.

WHAT WILL IT TAKE TO GET YOU OUT OF MY STRAW?
UNGH...

YOU'VE FAILED US, BRUCE!
YOU ALWAYS HAVE!
NO...!

I WON'T FAIL THEM-- NOT AGAIN!
STAY AWAY...!

YOU KNOW WHAT'S UNDER MY MASK--WHY DON'T YOU RETURN THE FAVOR!
DON'T--!
WHAT WERE YOU AFRAID I'D SEE? YOU'RE BEAUTIFUL!
AM I...?

...TAKE A SECOND LOOK!

SOB

SINCLAIR--!
BATMAN...
I KNEW YOU WEREN'T DEAD. BUT...

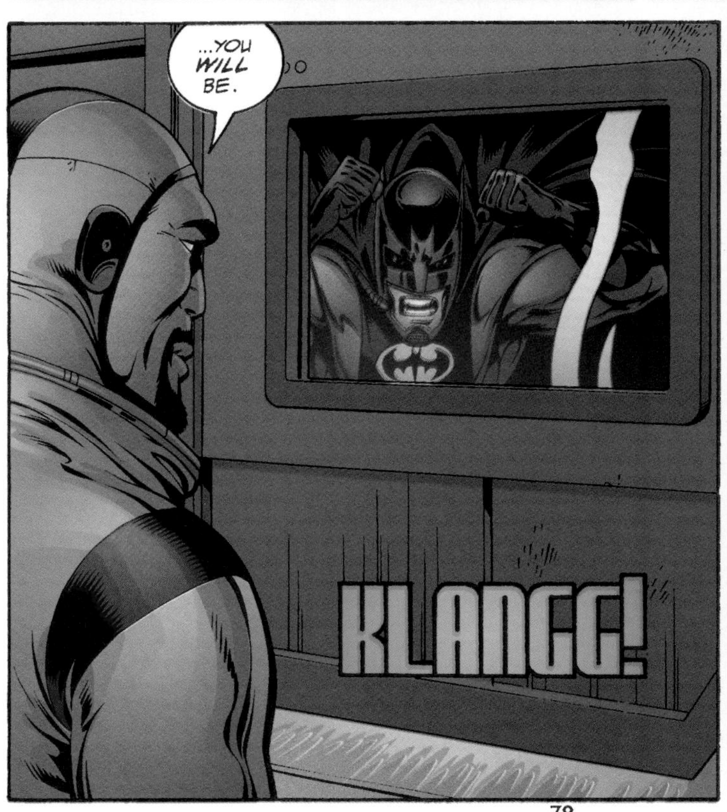
...YOU WILL BE.
KLANGG!

FAREWELL, BRUCE! GIVE MY REGARDS TO THE MAN IN THE MOON.

DEAD--!

UNLESS...
UNCONTAINED FIRE. INSTITUTING EMERGENCY VACUUM IN 5-- 4--

2--1--

PA-WHOOOOSH

I MIGHT HAVE KNOWN--!

VALENTIN, YOU MURDERED MY PARENTS--YOU'LL SPILL ALL THIS BLOOD--FOR A METEOR? WHY?
I HAVE ENOUGH TIME TO EXPLAIN--BUT YOU DON'T HAVE ENOUGH TIME TO HEAR!
DON'T--!

THERE--!

NO--!

NO...

IF WE CAN REACH THE SHUTTLE...RESTORE ITS POWER--
NO!

VALENTIN, HELP ME! YOU'LL DIE, TOO!

BUT NOT FOR LONG!

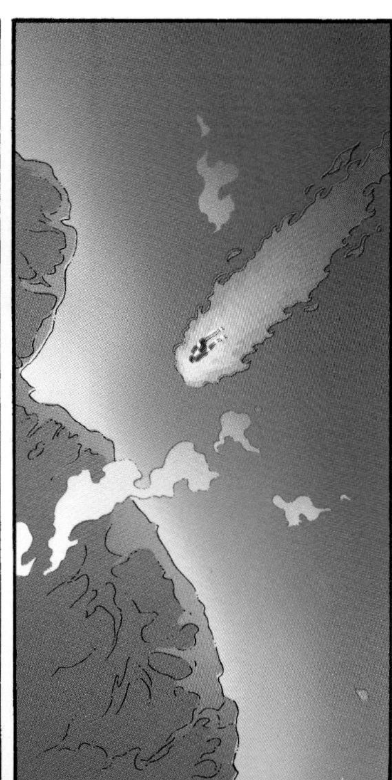

A SHOOTING STAR...! I WISH...

...I WISH...THAT BRUCE WILL COME HOME TO ME SOON!
1001 NAMES FOR THE BABY

I WIN AGAIN.
BUT THEN, I ALWAYS DO.

DARK FUTURE

A.D. 2500...

I THINK THIS IS *IT*..! GET IN WITH THAT *PROBE*...

CRKKK

YOU'RE NOT GOING *IN* THERE, MISS WAYNE?

ARE YOU *KIDDING*?

BRUCE WAYNE'S *STUDY!* I *KNEW* THE OLD MAPS WERE RIGHT!

SIX MONTHS LATER...
...AND SO, TO CELEBRATE THE SECOND HALF OF THE MILLENNIUM, WAYNE UNIVERSAL DEDICATES FOR THE PEOPLE OF LOWER GOTHAM, THE NEWLY-DISCOVERED REMNANTS OF WAYNE MANOR, WHICH --
MY SUIT!
SHPLATTT
DAMN LOW DOWNS --! CAN'T GIVE THEM ANYTHING --!
WELL, OF COURSE THEY'RE INDIGNANT, JAMES. WE LIVE IN LUXURY, HIGH ABOVE THEM, IN UPPER GOTHAM. THEY LIVE HERE, IN LOWER GOTHAM, IN FILTH, WITH INSUFFICIENT FOOD AND POLLUTED AIR...
...BESIDES --
-- THE SECOND HALF OF THE MILLENNIUM DOESN'T BEGIN UNTIL NEXT YEAR!
WE NEED FOOD!
KEEP BACK, YOU!

THANKS FOR HOLDING THE DOOR, JAMES!
PRESIDENTS FIRST, VICE-PRESIDENTS SECOND! BESIDES, I'M THE OLDER BROTHER, I --
DENIZENS OF UNDERGOTHAM, CEASE YOUR TRAVAILS...
WHO'S THAT?
I'VE HEARD ABOUT HIM, BUT I THOUGHT HE WAS A MYTH..!
...YOU HATE THE INTRUDERS FROM UPPERGOTHAM, AND RIGHTLY SO, BUT THEY WILL REPAY YOUR VIOLENCE TENFOLD!
THE PROPHET!
JOSHUA!
RETURN TO YOUR HOMES AND AWAIT MY WORDS! DELIVERANCE SHALL BE YOURS, WHEN COSMIC FIRE AGAIN APPROACHES THE EARTH!
BRENNA, ARE PROJECTS LIKE THESE ALL YOU SPEND YOUR TIME ON?
WHY DO THESE PEOPLE SMELL SO BAD, BRENNA? WHY DON'T THEY BUILD DECENT PLACES TO LIVE, LIKE WE DO?
I DON'T KNOW, JAMES...

...MAYBE THEY NEVER HEARD THE STORY OF THE TOWER OF BABEL.

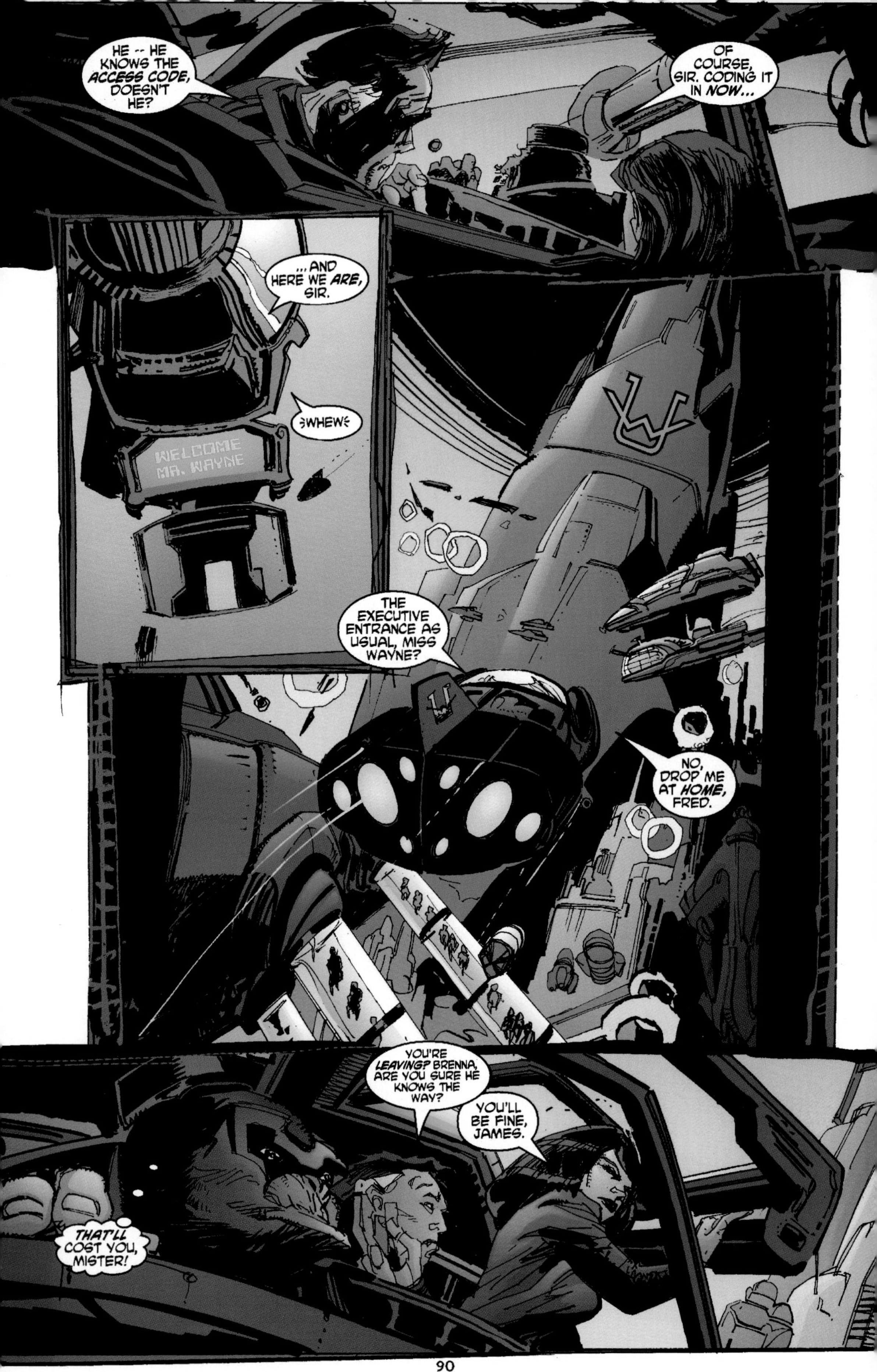
HE -- HE KNOWS THE ACCESS CODE, DOESN'T HE?
OF COURSE, SIR. CODING IT IN NOW...
...AND HERE WE ARE, SIR.
WELCOME MR. WAYNE
WHEW
THE EXECUTIVE ENTRANCE AS USUAL, MISS WAYNE?
NO, DROP ME AT HOME, FRED.
YOU'RE LEAVING? BRENNA, ARE YOU SURE HE KNOWS THE WAY?
YOU'LL BE FINE, JAMES.
THAT'LL COST YOU, MISTER!

GOOD AFTERNOON, MISS WAYNE. BEAUTIFUL DAY, ISN'T IT?
THEY ALWAYS *ARE*, CHARLIE.
I LEFT SOME MESSAGES...
YOU HAVE 373 MESSAGES AND/ OR HOLO-FAXES.
ANY FROM MY *BROTHER?*
TWENTY-NINE.
DELETE THOSE.
YOU HAVE 344 MESSAGES AND/OR --
RODNEY? RODNEY, WHERE ARE YOU?
HOW'D YOU GET DOWN *THERE?*
THE SCREEN'S NOT CODED TO ADMIT *YOU*.
DOWN HERE, BRENNA!

I OVERRODE IT! THAT'S WHY YOU ENHANCED ME, ISN'T IT? TO DO ALL THIS TECHNICAL STUFF? SO YOU CAN GET YOUR REVENGE?
WELL... YEAH...
IT'S NOT "REVENGE," IT'S SELF-PRESERVATION! YOU RESEARCHED ALL THESE GENERATIONS OF WAYNES, DIDN'T YOU? AS I TOLD YOU TO?
AND DIDN'T WE FIND THEY ALL DIED YOUNG? AND VIOLENTLY --?
-- AND DIDN'T WE FIND THAT THEY ALL WORE SOME KIND OF WEIRD "BAT-COSTUME" IN THEIR LAST DAYS? DO YOU THINK THAT COULD POSSIBLY BE COINCIDENCE?

OKAY, NO NEED TO BITE MY HEAD --
OKAY, I'M SORRY I ASKED!

I MANAGED TO CRACK THAT DISK YOU FOUND IN *WAYNE MANOR!* BOY, IT WAS *OLD.* WHO'S *THIS* GUY?
I DON'T KNOW...
I >KRZZT< *ALFRED PENNYWORTH*, GENTLE >ZKKZT< TO MR. *BRUCE* >KRZZT< HE HAS INSTRUCTED ME TO MAKE THIS >KZZZZZZZT<
RODNEY, I NEED THAT *BACK!*
I WAS LUCKY TO GET *THAT*, BRENNA! BUT I GOT *THIS* TOO...
...*HERE'S* AN OLDIE, BUT A GOODIE!
THAT *ENERGY SIGNATURE* AGAIN? THIS IS THE *EARLIEST* RECORD WE HAVE OF IT YET! SEE IF YOU CAN *CLEAN IT UP*, WHILE I --
HEY, LOOK AT *THIS!*
INCOMING TRANSMISSION--
EYES ONLY TRIPLE ENCRYPT
WHAT --?

THAT WAS FAST! GOOD WORK, PAL!
BUT IT WASN'T ME...
"...IT'S A TRANSMISSION FROM WAYNE UNIVERSAL!"
THE ENERGY SIGNATURE POPPED ONTO OUR SENSORS ONLY MINUTES AGO, MISS WAYNE, SO WE ROUTED IT TO YOU, AS PER YOUR ORDERS. I SHOULD TELL YOU...
...I APPRECIATE THAT YOU ALWAYS KEEP UP WITH OUR RESEARCH. MR. WAYNE BARELY EVEN KNOWS WE'RE HERE.
MY BROTHER AND I HAVE VERY DIFFERENT INTERESTS, DOCTOR. THIS ENERGY SIGNATURE CAME FROM A METEOR, YOU SAY?
IT JUST ENTERED THE RANGE OF OUR SATELLITES MINUTES AGO.
AND THAT RADIATION EMANATING FROM IT -- IS IT HARMFUL?
DIFFICULT TO GAUGE ITS EFFECTS WITHOUT FURTHER ANALYSIS. IF WE STILL HAD A SPACE PROGRAM...
MY BROTHER CALLS THAT A "FRIVOLOUS LUXURY" -- ANOTHER DIFFERENCE BETWEEN US. BUT --

"-- HE IS THE BOSS."
WAS I RIGHT, RODNEY?
I FOUND A TAP INTO THE WAYNE UNIVERSAL COMPUTER, ALL RIGHT, BRENNA...
...HOW'D YOU KNOW?
THIS "PROPHET" KNEW "COSMIC FIRE" -- THE METEOR -- WAS HERE ALMOST BEFORE WE DID! HE HAD TO HAVE INSIDE INFORMATION.
WHOEVER'S BEHIND HIM HAS PLAGUED MY FAMILY FOR GENERATIONS...
...BUT IT ENDS WITH ME -- THOUGH NOT IN A WAY THE OTHER SIDE WILL LIKE! READY FOR A LITTLE DRIVE?
AFTER ALL THE TRAINING WE'VE DONE? BOY, YOU BET..!
...CAN WE WEAR THE COSTUMES?
FIRST THINGS FIRST. AIRCAR TO COMBAT MODE, RODNEY.
CHECK!
WHURRR
NOW CAN WE WEAR THE COSTUMES?
COMBAT GEAR, RODNEY...

ALL RIGHT!

LET'S GO.
HEY, THIS IS KINDA FUN!
I KNOW, BUT REMEMBER --
"...WE HAVE SERIOUS BUSINESS BELOW."
YOU OF UNDERGOTHAM, HEAR MY WORDS AND HEED THEM -- LONG HAVE YOU HEARD MY WORDS AND BELIEVED, ON FAITH ALONE, AND YOU ARE BLESSED FOR IT...
...NOW IS YOUR FAITH REWARDED. NOW HAS COME THE MESSENGER FROM THE ETERNAL BEYOND, AS I FORETOLD -- YOUR HERALD OF A BETTER LIFE -- LIFE IMMORTAL!
THAT TAP ON THE WAYNE UNIVERSAL COMPUTER STOPS HERE, BOSS!
SO THIS "PROPHET" IS MIXED UP IN THIS! LET'S GET CLOSER SO WE CAN --

INTRUDERS!
UH OH!
CLEANSE THEM WITH THE PROPHET'S FLAME!
FWOOSH
FSST
I HATE THE SMELL OF BURNING HAIR -- ESPECIALLY MINE!
HEADS, I WIN...
...TAIL, YOU LOSE!
AGGH--!

LOOKS LIKE WE KINDA BLEW OUR *ENTRANCE.*
DOESN'T MATTER -- *GET* THE *PROPHET!*
RNNNCH
HOLD ON, BOSS, I'M --
RRAAKKK! AAAKK!
KLIK
SIT *TIGHT,* PAL!
WAK
VROOOM

PWOOM
WOOOM
MY REVELATION HAS BEEN DEFILED! LET US LEAVE THESE FAITHLESS!
AAAKK!
OOOOKK!
RODNEY! HERE --!
HEY, IT'S OKAY, PAL...
AAAKK!
OOOOKK!
B-BOSS? WOW, SORRY I DOWNGRADED FOR A SECOND THERE!
THAT'S OKAY, PARTNER...

...YOU'RE ONLY *HUMAN!*

THE DEFILERS HAVE *GONE,* MY PROPHET!

FOR THE NONCE. BUT THEY SHALL *RETURN,* AS SURELY AS *SUNRISE*...

...UNLESS I MAKE MY WILL KNOWN *FIRST* -- AND *HARSHLY.*

OH, REAL FUNNY! THAT'S SPECIST TALK, YOU KNOW! I COULD BRING YOU UP ON CHARGES BEFORE THE ANIMAL BOARD!
MY, DON'T WE HAVE HAIR ON OUR CHEST?

LOOK, KIDDO. I DIDN'T THINK... I SHOULD HAVE KNOWN... I MEAN, THIS IS MY FIGHT. YOU'RE A BIG HELP, BUT YOU DON'T HAVE TO GET INVOLVED ANYMORE IF YOU DON'T WANT TO.
NO WAY, LADY --

-- NOT UNTIL I GET MY PAWS ON THE CREEPS WHO PUT MY TAIL IN A SLING!
THEY MAY GET THEIR HANDS ON US FIRST, RODNEY. I MADE A VERY SERIOUS TACTICAL ERROR -

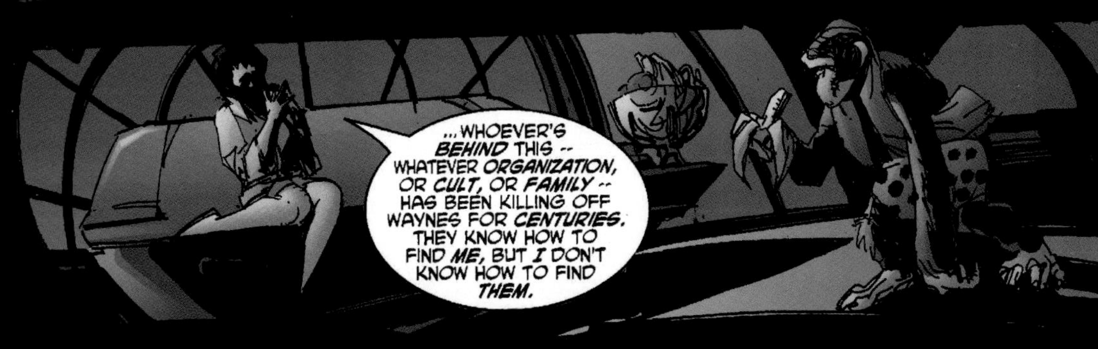
...WHOEVER'S BEHIND THIS -- WHATEVER ORGANIZATION, OR CULT, OR FAMILY -- HAS BEEN KILLING OFF WAYNES FOR CENTURIES. THEY KNOW HOW TO FIND ME, BUT I DON'T KNOW HOW TO FIND THEM.

BUT NOW THEY KNOW WE'RE ON TO THEM, SO --

KRACOOM
"WE ARE GATHERED HERE TODAY TO MOURN BRENNA WAYNE..."

MY SISTER LOVED BOTH GOTHAMS AND SPENT HER LIFE TRYING TO BRING THEM TOGETHER... THE TRAGIC ACCIDENT THAT TOOK HER LIFE HAS TOO SOON ENDED ALL THAT...
PLEASE, MA'AM, CAN YOU HELP..?
JONTRO! JONTRO, WHAT ARE YOU DOING?
NEVER BEG FROM OUR OWN KIND! WE HAVE SOME PRIDE!
IT'S ALL RIGHT -- I'VE HAD SOME WORK THIS WEEK, I CAN SPARE IT. ESPECIALLY IF YOU CAN TELL ME WHERE "THE PROPHET" LIVES.
THE PROPHET? I GO TO JOIN HIM, LEST WE DIE IN POVERTY. HIS PRIESTS HAVE SANCTIFIED ME AND GIVEN ME THIS AMULET...
INDEED? MAY I MAKE A PROPOSITION?

AWAY, WOMAN!
HAIL THE PROPHET! I HAVE COME TO JOIN YOUR HOLY ORDER AND SERVE JOSHUA!
AWAY! YOU ARE TOO LATE!
BUT I'VE BEEN CALLED --! THIS AMULET IS PROOF OF --
IT'S NO USE! WE CHOOSE WHO ENTERS, AND WHO DOES NOT!
I BEG YOU TO RECONSIDER!
WHUD
AGGG!
ON SECOND THOUGHT, THERE MAY BE A ROLE IN THE PROPHET'S RANKS FOR ONE SO... ER... STRONG IN THE FAITH...
I PRAISE YOUR ENLIGHTENMENT.

SERGEANT, ISSUE THIS CHOSEN ONE A UNIFORM AND BEGIN HER STUDIES!
YES, GUARDSMAN!
CHOSEN ONE -- YOU PASSED THE PHYSICAL JUST FINE -- BUT THERE'S A MORE IMPORTANT TEST TO PROVE YOU'RE WORTHY OF THE PROPHET'S SERVICE...
AND THAT WOULD BE..?
YOU MUST STUDY AND MEDITATE ON THE PROPHET'S TEACHINGS FOR SEVEN HOURS. AT THAT TIME, I WILL RETURN.
NOT FOR SEVEN HOURS? TOO BAD...
...I WAS HOPING YOU AND I COULD STUDY TOGETHER, HANDSOME!
ALL SUCH MATCHES ARE APPROVED BY THE PROPHET HIMSELF! I CANNOT --
THEN THINK IT OVER FOR AWHILE!
CRZZZT
UNHHH

GOOD. THEY WON'T BE LOOKING FOR ME FOR A LONG TIME...
...SO I CAN SNOOP A LITTLE -- WITH THE AID OF THIS ALL-ACCESS PASS!
HAIL JOSHUA!
HAIL THE PROPHET!
IT WOULD HELP IF I HAD SOME IDEA WHERE I WAS GOING...
NICE OF THEM TO MAKE IT SO EASY FOR ME!
SENIOR ACOLYTES ONLY
WELCOME, ACOLYTE, TO THE HALL OF THE PROPHET!
THAT SOUNDS INFORMATIVE...

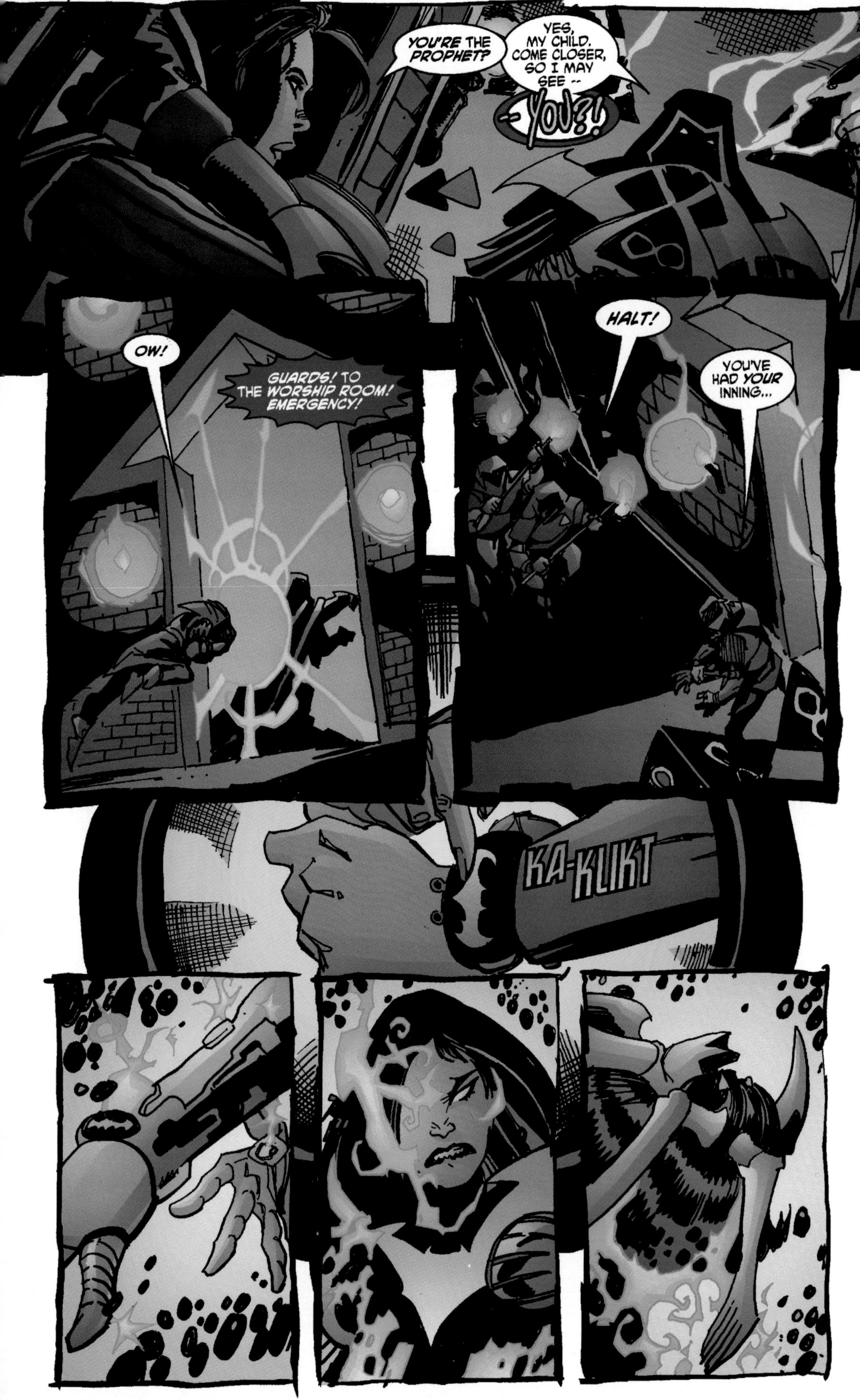
YOU'RE THE PROPHET?
YES, MY CHILD. COME CLOSER, SO I MAY SEE --
--YOU?!
OW!
GUARDS! TO THE WORSHIP ROOM! EMERGENCY!
HALT!
YOU'VE HAD YOUR INNING...
KA-KLIKT

...NOW IT'S MY TURN AT BAT!
"...WAIT FOR WORD FROM ME. THAT'S AN ORDER. WAIT FOR WORD FROM ME. THAT'S AN ORDER..!"
ACTIVATION
MISSED ME!
SPLRRSH
ZZPDT

NOW IT'S YOUR TURN, PROPHET!
SHAKRRSSH
HE WAS JUST A HOLOGRAM.
WHY AM I NOT SURPRISED..?
COMPUTER, TRACE SOURCE OF HOLOGRAPHIC ENERGY...
THANK YOU.
WORSHIPPED ONE, THE WAYNE HAS ESCAPED. SHOULD WE --?
ALL IS AS I HAVE FORESEEN...

"...PROCEED AS I HAVE DECREED."
HALT, OR --
WOOM
CRZZZT
ZDDDT
GOING DOWN..!
NOW WHERE AM I?
A TRANSPLANTED CAVE PAINTING..? OF A MAN BEING STRUCK BY A GLOWING THING FROM THE SKY -- A METEOR? -- WHO OUTLIVES EVERYONE AROUND HIM..!
...I'VE ALWAYS THOUGHT A CONSPIRACY, OR A SECRET SOCIETY WAS BEHIND THE WAR ON THE WAYNES... BUT ONE MAN? HE'D HAVE TO BE --
WELCOME, MISS WAYNE. I CONGRATULATE YOUR RESOURCEFULNESS.

YOU'RE "THE PROPHET"?
I AM.
THEN YOU'RE HISTORY.
CRACOOOM
V-VERY GOOD, MISS WAYNE...
...ALL YOUR ANCESTORS...
...WOULD BE PROUD.
YOU'RE NOT... YOU CAN'T BE...
YOU SAID IT YOURSELF, MISS WAYNE -- I AM HISTORY. I AM IMMORTAL. BUT SHOULD YOU NEED MORE TANGIBLE EVIDENCE...
...PLEASE TURN TO YOUR LEFT.
HIM --?!

BRRT
HIM. IN MUCH THE SAME STATE YOU'LL SOON BE.
WHAT HAVE YOU DONE --?
empty
MERELY MADE YOUR ARMOR OF NO MORE USE THAN IT WOULD HAVE BEEN WHEN I INVENTED ARMOR.
THIS, OF COURSE, IS A GAS OF MY INVENTION. I DON'T THINK IT'S FATAL.
SLEEP WELL.
UNHHH
HSSSSST
I... I KNOW IT'LL GIVE YOU NO END OF SATISFACTION, BUT -- "WHERE AM I?!"

YOU ARE SUSPENDED BETWEEN TWO OF UPPER GOTHAM'S ANTIGRAVITY GENERATORS. THEIR FORCES BIND YOUR ARMOR, SINCE ANTIGRAV DOES NOT AFFECT ORGANIC MATTER.
I SEE. THANK YOU.
OH, COME. BE GRACIOUS IN DEFEAT. BESIDES, GIVEN YOUR OBVIOUS INTEREST IN YOUR HERITAGE, YOU MUST HAVE MORE QUESTIONS.
WELL, I'D GUESS THOSE TRANSPORTS ARE CARRYING YOUR FORCES, SET TO TAKE OVER UPPERGOTHAM -- OR AT LEAST RECALIBRATE ITS GENERATORS.
AH, BUT DON'T YOU WANT TO KNOW WHY?
WELL, YOU CERTAINLY SEEM OBSESSED WITH THAT METEOR. YOU PLAN TO USE UPPERGOTHAM'S ANTIGRAV GENERATORS TO CAPTURE IT, RIGHT? DESPITE HOW MANY PEOPLE THAT WILL KILL.
YOURSELF INCLUDED. I AM IMPRESSED, MISS WAYNE. YOU DO YOUR FAMILY PROUD.
I SUPPOSE SO...
...EVEN THE BLACK SHEEP. RIGHT, JAMES?
HOW DID YOU --?
JAMES, PLEASE, SURELY IT WAS OBVIOUS...
...HOW ELSE COULD I HAVE OBTAINED A TAP ON THE WAYNE UNIVERSAL COMPUTER SYSTEM AS WELL AS THE ACCESS CODES OF HER APARTMENT BUILDING? WAS JAMES SIMPLY A BUNGLER, OR IS THERE SOME CLEVERER REASON WHY YOU SURVIVED MY EXPLOSIVE DEVICE?
I REALIZED IF I COULD DETECT YOUR TAP, YOU COULD DETECT ME... THE REST WAS BODY ARMOR, FORCE FIELDS AND WAITING.

BUT I HAVE TO ADMIT I WAS SURPRISED WHEN I FINALLY TUMBLED ON TO YOU, JAMES! WHAT DID HE OFFER YOU TO BETRAY YOUR FAMILY? MONEY? YOU'VE GOT ALL YOU'LL EVER NEED!
ALL THE MONEY, YES...
...BUT NOW THE NAME WILL BE MINE, ONLY MINE! DO YOU KNOW WHAT IT'S LIKE BEING THE "OTHER WAYNE"? DAMN IT! I'M THE ONE WHO'S PRESIDENT! I DID WHAT I HAD TO DO.
COME, JAMES, WE HAVE WORK.
TELL THAT TO FIFTY GENERATIONS OUR ANCESTORS!
JUST LIKE THAT? YOU'VE BEEN KILLING MY FAMILY FOR CENTURIES! WHY? JUST FOR THAT ROCK?
MISS WAYNE, "THAT ROCK" -- MORE SPECIFICALLY, THE ENERGY SIGNATURE IT EMITS -- MADE ME WHAT I AM. I KNOW IT IS THE CAUSE, BUT NOT THE REASON WHY.
"WHY"? FOR THE SAME REASON MILLIONS DIE IN A DISASTER, BUT ONE SURVIVES! DESTINY? FATE? LUCK?
MORE! THERE IS A REASON FOR MY LONGEVITY -- AND IT'S LOCKED INSIDE THAT ROCK! I POSSESSED IT, TASTED IT ONCE, FIVE CENTURIES AGO!
YOUR ANTECEDENTS HAVE CONTINUALLY THWARTED ME, BUT NOW I WIN! I ALWAYS WIN!
BUT WHY "JOSHUA"? IS THAT EVEN YOUR REAL NAME?
NO -- "VANDAL SAVAGE" -- A COGNOMEN I RARELY USE. IT REPRESENTS WHAT I WAS, NOT WHAT I AM. AS FOR "JOSHUA," I WAS RATHER FOND OF HIM. OF ALL OF YOU, REALLY. BUT YOU CROSSED ME.
GOODBYE, MISS WAYNE. WHEN I RECALIBRATE THE GENERATORS, YOU WILL DIE.
AND UPPER-GOTHAM WITH YOU.

WE'LL JUST SEE. IF IT'S THE ARMOR THE ANTIGRAV IS HOLDING, THEN..!
TAKE THEM! THEY'RE JUST BEASTS!
GRAVITY GENERATOR
HAIL, PROPHET! I PRAYED I WOULD LIVE TO WITNESS THIS MOMENT!
DO YOU KNOW WHAT DIOGENES TOLD ME ON HIS DEATHBED? HE SAID, "BURY ME ON MY FACE...
"...BECAUSE IN A LITTLE WHILE, EVERYTHING WILL BE TURNED UPSIDE DOWN."
AH --!
KLAK
I HOPE THIS WAS A GOOD IDEA..!

KLIK KLIK KLIK KLIK
COME ON, ARMOR... REACTIVATE! COME ON..!
ZMMMMMMMMM
YA GOTTA WATCH THAT FIRST STEP, BOSS!
RODNEY! THANK HEAVEN --
GOOD WORK, PAL! PUT IT IN REVERSE AND LET'S GET BACK UPSTAIRS BEFORE --
UH, BRENNA..? IF YOU WERE GONNA SAY "BEFORE IT'S TOO LATE..."
...IT'S TOO LATE!
AIEE!

VERY GOOD, MY ACOLYTES! JAMES, IF YOU'LL EXCUSE ME --? THIS IS A RATHER PERSONAL MOMENT.
AT LAST!
NOW IT'S OUR TURN TO WALK IN THE SKY!
THIS IS ALL WE HAVE? THE ANTIQUE?
AFRAID SO.
ANY OLD PORT IN A STORM --!
RRRRRT
SHNNG
RRRRRT
SHNNG
THE ANTINERTIAL FIELD OUGHT TO KEEP THE CITIZENS FROM FALLING OUT OF THE CITY FOR ABOUT FIFTEEN MINUTES. YOU'VE GOT THAT LONG TO RIGHT THE GRAVITY, PAL. I'VE GOT TO STOP SAVAGE!
I ALWAYS WANTED TOP BILLING!

THERE IT IS!
IT'S MINE...
...MINE...
SAVAGE.
NO.
RELEASE THAT METEOR!
ZNNT

IT WON'T DO, MISS WAYNE. I'VE WANTED THIS METEOR FOR MORE YEARS THAN YOU'VE HAD ANCESTORS.
AND IT'S ABOUT TO BECOME THAT MANY PIECES!
NO!
ONLY ONE WAY TO RALLY THESE PALOOKAS! HATE TO DO THIS TO THE BIG GUYS...
>SNFF< HKKKK?
RAAKK GRAAAHHH
...BUT IF FIRE MAKES ME GO FERAL --!
DO YOU HEAR --?
OH, GOOD GOD.

AW, NO! SAYS HERE THAT CONTROL OF THE GRAVITY FIELD HAS BEEN TRANSFERRED TO SAVAGE! IT'S UP TO BRENNA TO OVERRIDE IT -- AND SOON!
DO YOU SEE, MISS WAYNE? DO YOU REALIZE THE FUTILITY OF YOUR ACTS?
LOOK WHO'S TALKING -- IT'S BEEN FIVE HUNDRED CENTURIES SINCE YOU BECAME IMMORTAL! IF IT WAS MORE THAN CHANCE, WOULDN'T YOU KNOW IT BY NOW?
BUT THE UNIVERSE IS ETERNAL, IT'S PATIENT...
YOU'RE ETERNAL, SAVAGE...
SRRRRRT
...BUT YOU'RE NOT PATIENT!
A -- A BALLISTIC WEAPON? HOW CHARMINGLY ATAVISTIC...!

...AND HOW USELESS!
OUT OF AMMO -- BUT HIS FIELD DIDN'T STOP BULLETS...
KLIK KLIKK
...AND IT MIGHT NOT STOP THIS...
YOU'VE SEEN YOUR BEST WEAPONRY FAIL AGAINST ME! DO YOU THINK THAT WILL FARE ANY BETTER?
...BUT I'M NOT AIMING AT HIM!
DON'T --!
KRZZZZT
ZKKKKT
KRMMMMM
YIKES --!
THE CITY'S GOING DOWN!

SAVAGE, COME ON --!
I'M AFRAID NOT, MISS WAYNE...
...LIFE'S TOO LONG TO DENY MYSELF WHAT I'VE ALWAYS WANTED -- ANSWERS THAT ONLY THIS METEOR CAN GIVE ME --
-- WHO AM I? WHY AM I?
WHAT GOOD WILL THOSE ANSWERS DO YOU, DRIFTING IN OUTER SPACE?
SPOKEN LIKE A TRUE MORTAL...
WHOA...
SKRKKKK
KRNK
KRKK
KRNNK

HMMMMMMMMMM
RODNEY --!
KRSSSSSH
WHEW
SOME DAYS
I WISH I'D NEVER
LEFT THE
JUNGLE!

BRENNA? BRENNA?
RIGHT HERE, RODNEY!
ARE YOU OKAY? WHERE'S SAVAGE?
ASK ME AGAIN IN ANOTHER FIVE HUNDRED YEARS! WHERE'S JAMES?
WELL... THERE'S NOT MUCH LEFT OF HIM...
UNFORTUNATELY -- THERE WAS NEVER MUCH TO HIM.
AND NOW WE'RE EARTHBOUND! THE CITY COUNCIL IS GONNA BE SO MAD...!
LET THEM! THIS IS THE WAY IT USED TO BE. MAYBE THIS IS THE WAY IT'S SUPPOSED TO BE.
AND HOW ABOUT YOU? YOU OKAY?
BETTER THAN THAT. FOR THE FIRST TIME IN THIRTEEN CENTURIES, THE WAYNE FAMILY IS FREE. FOR THE FIRST TIME IN MY LIFE...
...I'VE GOT TOMORROW.

UNDERGOTHAM
[Ref. Pg 4]
CUT-AWAY VIEW
FILTHY, OPAQUE SHELL
SOME BLDGS JUT THRU SHELL
HAPHAZARD PARTIAL LAYERS (typ).
ORIGINAL GND LEVEL
(WHERE WAYNE MANOR RUINS ARE FOUND)
[Ref. 7-8]
NO SUNLIGHT
STANDING HOLO IMAGE
HOLOGRAPHIC SCREEN (typ.)
BATWOMAN COSTUME DESIGNS
A
REF PAGE 12 DESC. (FORM-FITTING ARMOR)
B
REF PAGE 24 DESC. (EVEN COOLER ARMOR)
C
REF PAGE ?* DESC (MORE CLASSIC, LOW-TECH)
* ORIG SCRIPT PG. 36.
GORILLA CHARACTERS: [Ref Pg 3]
RIOT GEAR GUARD
CHAUFFEUR
SECURITY
(STD. GEAR)
A
B
C
COMPACT COMPUTER MODULE
REF PG. 12 DESC.
(CLASSIC ROBIN COSTUME)
except cape is black on outside, Yellow on inside.

VANDAL SAVAGE
POST-SEARING (Pg. 27)
APPEARANCE & GARB
(REVERTS TO CAVEMAN-LIKE APPEARANCE)
CIVILIAN/ STREET MODE
DEPLOYED IN BATTLE MODE
the PROPHET
[Ref. Pg 23]
WAYNE UNIVERSAL AIRCAR
WAYNE UNIVERSAL LOGO
ACOLYTE SEDAN CHAIR BEARERS
PYRAMID SHAPED AMULET w/ INFINITY SIGN
RUSTED LIMO FRAME/CAB
SEDAN CHAIR
DIAPHANOUS CURTAINS
PROPHET'S GUARD
[Ref Pg 20]
PROPHET'S SOLDIER
[Ref Pg 21]
TASER STAFF
TASER STICK
NOTE: BREAST EMBLEM FUNCTIONS AS A COMMUNICATOR. NIFTY!
Design sketches by Scott McDaniel